❀Simply Sarah❀

# Patches and Scratches

by **Phyllis Reynolds Naylor**

illustrated by **Marcy Ramsey**

Marshall Cavendish Children

To Aidan Saah
—P. R. N

Text copyright © 2007 by Phyllis Reynolds Naylor
Illustrations copyright © 2007 by Marshall Cavendish
First Marshall Cavendish paperback edition, 2010

Marshall Cavendish Corporation
99 White Plains Road, Tarrytown, NY 10591
www.marshallcavendish.us/kids

Library of Congress Cataloging-in-Publication Data
Naylor, Phyllis Reynolds.
Patches and scratches / by Phyllis Reynolds Naylor ; illustrated by Marcy Ramsey. — 1st ed.
p. cm. — (Simply Sarah)
Summary: Sarah, who is very good at solving problems, tries to help
her friend Peter find a pet that he and his grandmother both like.
ISBN-13: 978-0-7614-5347-5 (hardcover) 978-0-7614-5731-2 (paperback)
[1. Cats—Fiction. 2. Pets—Fiction. 3. Neighbors—Fiction.] I. Ramsey, Marcy Dunn, ill.
II. Title. III. Series.
PZ7.N24Pat 2007
[Fic]—dc22
2006026564

Book design by Vera Soki
The illustrations are rendered in ink and wash.

Printed in China (E)
A Marshall Cavendish Chapter Book
2 4 6 5 3 1

 Marshall Cavendish
Children

# Contents

## One

# Anything but Ordinary

Sarah Simpson wanted to be anything but ordinary. To be special, however, meant that she had to be good at something. And Sarah was very good at solving problems. Her father called her his "Idea Girl." All she needed were some problems to solve.

She lived with her mother and her younger brother, Riley. Their home was on the fourth floor of an apartment building in Chicago. Her mother was an artist who drew pictures for books.

"Do you have any problems for me to solve?" Sarah asked her mother.

"I have lots of problems," her mother told her. "I'm trying to draw a picture of a bear on a bicycle. That's a problem. I painted a picture of a boy with black hair. It should have been blond. That's a problem."

Sarah didn't know how to fix those kinds of problems, so she went to look for Riley. He was watching his favorite video, about a lion.

"Riley . . . ," Sarah whispered.

"Shhhh," said Riley.

She waited a minute or two.

"Riley," she whispered again. She jiggled his arm.

"*What?*" Riley grumbled, his eyes on the screen.

"Do you have any problems?" asked Sarah.

"Yes," said Riley. "You are my problem."

Sarah sighed. She went to the window to watch the pigeons that flew between the apartment buildings. The Simpsons' apartment was called a loft. It was on the

2

top floor and had a skylight in the roof to let in light. The rooms were made by bookcases and screens that stood in place of walls.

Mom worked at a big table. Dozens of pictures were propped all around her —pictures of raccoons and ships and monkeys. There were hundreds of paint specks on the floor—green and orange and black and violet.

Sarah's father worked overseas building bridges. He called home every Sunday to speak to his family. When he called this

Sunday, Sarah decided, she would ask if *he* had a problem. She couldn't help her father with a problem about bridges, but she could help with a problem about breakfast, maybe. Soggy pancakes or floppy bacon.

But when he called the next day, Sarah's father spent most of the time talking to Mom. He wanted to talk about vacations, and when he would see them again. When he talked to Sarah, he just said, "How are things going at school, Princess? Keep up the good work."

Sarah was not a princess. She certainly didn't want to be ordinary—but she didn't want to be *that*. Princesses had boring lives. They sat around all day with crowns on their heads, waiting for people to do things for them. Sarah liked to do things herself. She was, after all, the Idea Girl.

# Two

# What Peter Wanted

On the way home from school the next day, Sarah found a problem. It was her friend Peter's problem.

"I wish I could have a dog waiting for me when I get home," he said. "I've always wanted a dog."

"So why don't you get one?" asked Sarah.

"Granny Belle says no," said Peter.

Peter lived in the apartment below the Simpsons' with his grandmother. Sometimes he came upstairs to Sarah's when they got home from school. Sometimes two more

friends joined them, Mercedes and her cousin Leon. They lived in the building next door.

On this particular Monday they all sat around the table in Sarah's apartment drinking cocoa. Riley liked to sit with them. "The Cocoa Club," Sarah's mother called it.

"Peter wants a pet," Sarah told the others.

"A gerbil?" asked Leon.

Peter shook his head.

"A kitten?" asked Riley.

"No. I want a pet that will run with me and go where I go," said Peter.

"Get a horse," said Mercedes.

"How could I have a horse in the city?" Peter asked.

"A rabbit, then," said Leon.

"I want a dog," said Peter. "A dog that will do tricks and roll over and play dead."

Sarah thought how much fun it would be if Peter had a dog. They could take it for walks around the block and let it run in the park. "Why won't your grandmother let you have one?" she asked.

"I don't know," Peter answered.

"Then let's go ask," said Sarah. They all trooped down to Peter's apartment.

Granny Belle opened the door. "What do you think this is, a bus station?" she asked as the children filed in.

Granny Belle always had slippers on her feet, a sweater around her shoulders, and a smile on her face. Even when she was teasing. Today she had *two* sweaters over her shoulders, one on top of the other. It was fall, and the air outside was chilly.

"We came to talk to you about Peter," said Sarah. "He wants a dog."

Granny Belle sat down in her big, soft chair. The whole room was soft. There were soft rugs on the floor, soft pillows on the sofa, and soft curtains at the windows.

"Peter wants a lot of things we can't have," said Granny Belle. "A dog is one of them."

"Why *not*?" asked Peter.

"Because they make too much noise,"

said his grandmother.

"What about a kitten?" asked Riley.

"It would get hair all over the sofa pillows," said Granny Belle.

"A rabbit?" asked Leon.

"Rabbits need a big cage," said Peter's grandmother.

"Hamsters?" said Mercedes.

"Too much like rats," said the old woman.

"A bird, then?" asked Sarah, wanting *something* for Peter to call his own. "A canary, maybe?"

But Peter didn't want a bird. "I want a dog to play with," he told her.

"Peter, you listen now," said his grandmother. "It's a big decision to get a pet."

"Why?" asked Peter. "What can be so hard about going out and buying a dog?"

"Because you are buying a bark," said Granny Belle. "You are buying a mess. You are buying a smell. You might even be buying a bite. Who would feed it?"

"I would," said Peter.

"Who would walk it?"

"I would," said Peter.

"Who would give it baths and clean up its mess? I don't think pets are even allowed in this building. Have you heard one other bark coming from these apartments? Have you heard any squeaks or squawks or meows?"

"Let's find out!" Sarah said. "Let's go down and talk to Mr. Gurdy. *He'll* tell us if pets are allowed in this building."

And down the stairs they went.

## Three

# Mr. Gurdy

"No!" said Mr. Gurdy, when he saw them coming.

*No* was his favorite word.

"You don't even know what we're going to ask!" said Sarah.

"It's still NO with a capital *N*," said the man with the handlebar mustache.

Mr. Gurdy took care of the building. He lived in a room in the basement. The steam pipes hissed all around him. The water tanks dripped. The fans hummed and the furnace clanked. But inside Mr. Gurdy's room, it was cozy and warm. The man with the great gray

11

mustache sat in his favorite chair with his feet on a pillow. He was having his afternoon rest.

"I came to ask if I could have a dog in our apartment," said Peter.

Mr. Gurdy rolled his eyes beneath his shaggy eyebrows. "Absolutely not."

"I won't let it bother anyone," said Peter.

"No way!" said Mr. Gurdy.

"I'll clean up its mess. It won't get your floor dirty," promised Peter.

"N-O!" said Mr. Gurdy. "It's in the lease. No dogs allowed."

"What about kittens, Mr. Gurdy?" Sarah asked hopefully. How could she solve this problem if the only word people could say was *no*?

Mr. Gurdy pretended he hadn't heard. He got up from his chair and started to whistle. He reached for a bucket and mop and went out into the hallway.

"What about rabbits?" asked Leon.

Mr. Gurdy whistled even louder. "Can't

hear! Can't hear!" he called, and began to mop the floor.

"Lizards, snakes, rats, hamsters, or parrots?" asked Mercedes.

Mr. Gurdy began to sing.

"Mr. Gurdy!" Sarah shouted. "Does the lease say anything about other kinds of pets?"

At last Mr. Gurdy stopped singing. He stopped mopping.

"No," he said with a sigh. "There is nothing in the rules about lizards, snakes, rats, hamsters, parrots, salamanders, kittens, or rabbits."

"Hooray!" cried Sarah and Riley and Mercedes and Leon.

But that didn't help.

"I want a dog," Peter said. And that was a problem.

Mercedes and Leon went home. Peter went back to his apartment on the third floor. Sarah and Riley went on up to the loft.

14

Mom had painted a picture of three puppies sleeping in a basket to go on the cover of a book.

"How do you like it?" she asked, holding it up for them to see. "I just finished."

Sarah and Riley looked at the picture.

"It's sad," said Sarah.

"Sad?" asked Mom. "How can you call that sad? Three little puppies asleep in a basket."

"Because Peter can't have any of them," said Sarah. Somehow she *had* to help Peter get a pet.

In Mrs. Gold's class the following week, everyone was supposed to write a story called, "If I Was an Animal, What Would I Be?"

Sarah never chose anything ordinary, so she chose a monkey.

Peter, of course, chose a dog.

In art class, everyone was asked to draw a picture using only two colors.

Sarah drew a green bush with red berries. Peter drew a black dog with white spots.

It seemed as though wherever they looked, there was something to remind them of the dog Peter could not have.

For lunch, there were hot dogs. On the way home, Sarah shared a box of animal crackers with her friends. Emily Watson got a buffalo. Tim Wong got a cow. Sarah got a hippo, and Peter got a dog!

Sarah made up her mind. On Saturday, she would visit the pet store.

Sarah woke up early on Saturday. She ate her cereal, her eyes on the clock. When the hour hand got to ten, she took the money she kept in her sock drawer. She put it in her jacket pocket.

"Could I go up the street to the pet store?" she asked her mother.

"Is Peter going with you?" asked Mom.

"No. It would only make him sad," Sarah

said. "All he wants is a dog. I just want to see what they have."

"Then go right there and come right back," Mom told her. "Don't stop anyplace else."

"I won't," said Sarah. Riley was playing with his trucks. Sarah was glad. She wanted to think, not talk, on her way to the store.

It was a good thing that the pet store was up the block and around a corner because Sarah didn't have to cross any streets. She and Peter did not have to pass it on their way to school. That really would have made Peter sad.

When Sarah got to the pet store, she looked in the big window on one side of the entrance. There were four little kittens. In the big window on the other side, there were two little puppies, and Sarah went inside. She heard mewing and yipping. She heard parrots screeching from a perch up above. She heard hamsters riding a wheel in their cage. There was even a duck quacking in a

little pool at the back of the store.

"Hello," said the clerk. "May I help you? What are you looking for?"

"What I would really like is a dog to give my friend, but he can't have dogs in his apartment," said Sarah.

"How about a goldfish?" the woman suggested.

Sarah looked at the big tank of tropical fish. Some were big and blue and yellow. Some were small and orange. A tiny goldfish swam right along the side of the tank. Its little round mouth opened and closed, opened and closed. When the goldfish got to the end, it turned and swam back again.

"I'll take that one," Sarah said, pointing to the fish.

"Do you need a fishbowl, too?" asked the clerk. Sarah nodded.

"I would also like some colored rocks to put on the bottom, and a little cave the fish could hide in. How much would all that cost?" asked Sarah.

The clerk added the price of the bowl to the price of the goldfish. She added the prices of the rocks and the little cave. It took almost all of Sarah's money.

"Tell you what," said the clerk. "You will also need some fish food and a little green plant to go in the bowl. I'll let you have those for free."

"Thank you," said Sarah. She wished she felt happier about her gift to Peter.

The clerk put the rocks on the bottom of the bowl. Then she filled the bowl half full of water from the fish tank, and added the cave, rocks, and small green plant. She took a little net and gently scooped the small goldfish from the tank and placed it in the bowl.

The goldfish swam around and around. It went into the cave and hid for a second or two before it swam out again.

"I think it likes its new home," the clerk said, smiling.

"I hope that Peter likes the *fish*!" said Sarah.

"If he doesn't, you may bring it back. But it must be before the store closes at six o'clock," the woman said.

# Four

# Trying Again

Carefully, carefully, Sarah put the fish food in her pocket and took the bowl in her hands. The clerk held the door open as Sarah stepped outside. Then carefully, carefully, she walked along the sidewalk to the corner. She turned and went down the hill toward the apartments.

The mailman saw her coming and held the door open for her. When Sarah got to Peter's apartment, she tapped on the door with the toe of her shoe. *Bam, bam, bam.*

"I'm coming, I'm coming," called Granny Belle from inside. She opened the door and

stared at Sarah and the goldfish. Then she opened the door wider to let her in. "Good gracious," she said, one hand to her cheek.

Sarah carefully set the bowl on the table. Peter came in from the next room.

"Here's a pet that won't make any noise or mess, Peter," she told him. "It won't bark or bite. If you don't want it, though, I have to take it back to the store before six o'clock."

Peter didn't smile. He stared at the fish and the fish stared back. He put his face near the bowl, but the fish swam away.

Peter leaned over the bowl and called softly, "Goldie? Here, Goldie!" The fish didn't even look up.

Peter looked sad. "You're a good friend, Sarah," he said, "but I don't want a fish."


Sarah went upstairs to tell her mother she was taking the goldfish back.

"Oh, Sarah, that's too bad," Mom said. "But it was a nice thought."

"A nice thought doesn't solve the problem, though," said Sarah.

"Maybe that's a problem Peter has to solve," Mom said.

But Peter was Sarah's friend. The Idea Girl ought to be able to think of *something*, Sarah told herself.

"I want to go with Sarah," Riley said. "Maybe I can find something for Peter."

"Do you have any money?" Sarah asked.

Riley looked in his cement-mixer bank. He had two dollars and seven cents.

"Go right to the pet store and come right back," said their mother.

At the pet store, the woman took back the goldfish. "Do you see anything else your friend might like?" she asked.

Riley walked around and around. He picked up a kitten and rubbed noses. He let a dog lick his hand. He said hello to a parrot. Then he stopped at the turtle tank and watched the small turtles sitting under a sunlamp. They stretched their little necks toward the heat, opening and closing their eyes.

"I want to buy a turtle," he told the clerk.

"You'll need a place to keep it," the woman told him. "What about using this fishbowl? We'll pour out the water and put in some sand and a rock." She also gave him a little booklet about caring for a turtle.

Riley chose the turtle he wanted and carefully carried it out of the store.

"Remember," the clerk told him, "if your friend doesn't want it, you can return it. But you must bring it back before six tonight."

"We'll remember," said Sarah.

When Granny Belle opened the door this time, she said, "Goodness gracious, what are you doing? Robbing a zoo?"

"It's for Peter," said Riley. "In place of a dog." He went inside and set the fishbowl on the table.

"Not again!" said Peter. But then he saw the turtle. He sat down at the table and put

his face near the glass. "Hello, Turtle," he said softly. The turtle closed its eyes.

Peter reached into the fishbowl and gently picked up the little creature. He set it in the palm of his hand. The turtle drew in his head. He tucked his feet under him and disappeared into his shell.

Peter sadly shook his head. "Thanks," he said. "But please don't bring me any more pets. I only want a dog."

"I'm sorry," Granny Belle told the children.

Sarah and Riley took the turtle back to the pet store.

"I'm sorry," the clerk said, too. But she wasn't half as sorry as Sarah, the Idea Girl, who was running out of ideas very fast.

When Father called on Sunday, Sarah told him about Peter wanting a dog. "Did you ever want something you couldn't have?" she asked him.

"Yes," her father said. "When I was eighteen, I wanted a car, but I couldn't afford to buy one. So I had to make do with a bike until I'd saved enough money. When I finally got a car, I enjoyed it all the more."

"What if you didn't like your bike? What if all you wanted was a car or nothing?" Sarah asked.

"Then I guess I'd have to have settled for nothing," her dad said.

On Monday after school, Sarah and Peter walked home together as usual. The leaves on the trees had changed from green and gold to red and brown. The wind, which was only a little breeze a few days before, now tossed Sarah's hair. It made Peter pull up the hood of his jacket.

They went up the stairs to Sarah's loft. When Mercedes and Leon got off the Saint Mary's bus after school, they came over, too. They all sat down and had some cocoa. All but Peter. He just sat with his chin in his hands. The longer he went without a dog, it seemed, the more he wanted one.

The telephone rang. Sarah's mother answered.

"Yes," she said into the phone. "Peter's here. I'll send him right down." She turned to Peter. "Your grandmother wants you to come downstairs and bring your friends with you."

"Why?" asked Sarah.

"She didn't say," said Mom.

*A dog?* thought Sarah. Was it possible that Granny Belle had bought one for Peter after all? Was it going to be a surprise?

Sarah and Riley and Peter and Mercedes

and Leon hurried downstairs and opened the door to apartment number 303. There, sitting just inside the door, was a surprise, all right.

A cat with brown and white and black and yellow patches.

## Five

# The Surprise

The surprise gave a little meow.

Peter stared. Sarah stared.

"It's not a dog," said Peter.

"Well, it's a very special kind of dog. We call it a cat," joked Granny Belle. "Tim Wong's mother brought it by this afternoon. She said it's been hanging around their place. She said the last thing a restaurant needs is a cat jumping up on the tables."

Sarah thought of Wongs' Restaurant, with the two red dragons on either side of the front door. She thought of the big tank with the tropical fish in it. A restaurant did not need a cat sitting by a fish tank, either, dipping its paws in the water, trying to catch a fish.

"Why did Mrs. Wong bring it here?" Mercedes asked.

"Well, it seems that a girl named Sarah has been telling all her friends at school that Peter needs a pet," said Granny Belle. "Before you know it, we'll have rabbits and ducks and hamsters showing up at our door." Then she looked around at Mercedes and Leon. "I thought maybe one of *you* children would like to take this cat home."

Sarah wished she could solve this problem by taking the calico cat home herself, but she couldn't. "Mom's allergic to cats," she said.

Mercedes, too, was shaking her head. "There aren't any pets at all allowed in our building."

Granny Belle looked unhappy. So did Peter. The cat was rubbing against his legs, but Peter didn't pet her. Maybe, Sarah thought, she could help Peter *want* a cat.

She reached down and picked it up. The cat purred loudly, so loudly Sarah could feel the purr against her arms. It felt like a motor running inside the animal. She stroked the cat behind the ears, and it purred even louder.

"Try holding her, Peter," she said, handing the cat to him.

The cat scrambled out of Peter's arms and leaped to the floor.

"She scratched me!" Peter said.

"She didn't mean to," Sarah said. "She's just not used to us yet."

"Dogs don't scratch," said Peter. "I want a dog."

Mercedes and Leon kneeled down on the rug. Riley did, too.

Leon dug in his pocket and found a long piece of string. He began to pull it across the rug.

*Pounce!*

The cat jumped on the end of the string

and began to pull at it. Everyone laughed. Everyone but Peter and his grandmother.

"What are you going to name her, Peter?" Mercedes asked.

Peter only looked at the scratches on his arm. "She's not my cat," he said. "I wanted a dog."

"You could call her Scratches!" Riley said.

"You could name her Dog!" suggested Leon.

Peter finally sat down on the floor and watched the cat grabbing at the string.

"Her fur is just patches of white and brown and yellow and black," he said. "If she has to have a name, I guess it should be Patches." And he smiled just the teeniest, tiniest bit.

But Granny Belle was not happy, Sarah could tell. "Ask around at school, Peter, and see if you can't find someone there who will take her. We'll only keep her here until you find her a home," she said.

Sarah tapped on Peter's door the next morning on her way to school. Peter opened it. He had on two Band-Aids. One was on his arm. One was on his hand.

"She scratched me again," said Peter.

*Oh, no!* thought Sarah.

As they went downstairs, Peter said, "Patches did three things: she scratched me, she licked the butter off Granny Belle's toast, and she pooped on the rug. We had to buy her a litter box."

Sarah took a deep breath. She did not think that Patches would stay at Peter's place for very long. She wished someone would give her a problem she could *solve*.

"So you're going to give her away?" she asked as they went outside.

"Well, she did three *other* things, too," said Peter. "She ran after a ball, she sat in my lap, and she purred."

Maybe Patches would stay at Peter's place after all! Sarah thought.

Just in case, however, she went around to all their friends at recess and asked if anyone would like a cat. Tim Wong said no, of course.

"We already have a cat," said Emily Watson.

One friend had a dog who didn't like cats. Another had three cats and didn't need any more.

"It looks like nobody else wants her, Peter," Sarah said when the bell rang and everyone went back inside. "Maybe she'll have to be yours."

"I still want a dog," said Peter.

When school was out and they got back to Peter's apartment, Granny Belle looked cross. "Did you find someone to take this animal?" she asked.

Peter shook his head.

"That cat of yours ruined a good pair of my stockings today," she said. "She scratched a hole on one side."

"Uh-oh," said Sarah.

Patches came over to Peter and rubbed against his legs.

"Then she jumped up on the table and made off with a piece of my hamburger," Granny Belle complained.

Peter picked up Patches, and the cat began to purr.

"And that's not all!" said Peter's grandmother. "That animal left hair all over the couch and the rug."

Peter stroked the cat's head.

Granny Belle studied her grandson. "Peter Jefferson Grant!" she said. "I think you're beginning to like that cat."

## Six

# Going Crazy

"How do you make people like something?" Sarah asked her mother.

"You can't *make* anyone like anything," Mom said, putting a touch of paint on a picture of a ship at sea.

"Does that mean they won't like it ever?" asked Sarah.

"Well, you didn't like Mercedes and Leon very much when they first moved in next door," Mom told her.

"Because they made faces at us from their window," said Sarah, remembering.

"And what made you change your mind about them?"

Sarah thought about that a minute. "I invited them over," she said. "And after I got to know them, I liked them."

"Exactly," said Mom.

Perhaps Granny Belle and Peter just had to get to know Patches a little better, Sarah thought.

The next day, Sarah went to visit Peter. He certainly seemed to like the cat better. He was trying to teach Patches some tricks.

"Humph," said Granny Belle, looking up from the scarf she was knitting.

"Roll over," Peter said to the cat, which was stretched out on the rug. "Roll over, Patches." He nudged Patches with a yardstick.

Patches grabbed hold of the yardstick with her four paws and tried to bite it.

"That cat has a mind of her own," said Granny Belle, frowning. "She won't roll over

unless there's something to roll over *for*."

Peter took the yardstick away, and Patches lay quietly on her side. He sat down beside the cat. He stroked her head. Patches purred. Her eyes began to close.

Peter took a small rubber ball and put it behind Patches' back. He squeezed it and said, "Roll over, Patches."

*Squeak!* went the ball.

Patches rolled over and tried to catch it with her claws.

"Good cat! Good cat!" Peter said.

He put the little ball on the other side of Patches and squeezed it again.

"Roll over, Patches!" he said.

*Squeak!* went the ball.

Patches rolled over on her other side, grabbing for the ball.

"That's right! Good cat!" said Peter. He did it again. Each time he squeezed the ball, he said, "Roll over, Patches!" And each time the ball squeaked, Patches rolled over.

"See?" Peter said to Granny Belle. "She

41

already obeys when I say 'Roll over.'"

"Hogwash," said Granny Belle, and she went on with her knitting.

"Now teach her to play dead," said Sarah, grinning.

"That's easy," said Peter. He rubbed the cat's head until she lay very, very still. Her head began to sink down lower. Finally she stretched herself out flat against the floor in a spot of sunshine and went to sleep.

"Play dead, Patches," Peter whispered.

The cat didn't move.

"See?" said Peter. "She's playing dead."

"Hogwash," said Granny Belle.

"Do you want to see my cat jump?" Peter asked Sarah.

"Sure," Sarah said.

Peter went to the kitchen, and Sarah followed. He went over to the electric can opener.

"Watch Patches," Peter said, and they looked at the cat through the doorway. Even though there was no can to open, Peter pressed his hand against the lever of the can opener.

*Whirrrr*, went the can opener.

Instantly Patches leaped to her feet in the other room and came running out to the kitchen.

"Did you see her jump up?" asked Peter.

Sarah laughed. "She can do lots of tricks," she said. "She's even better than a dog."

"Her best trick is 'Going crazy,'" said Peter. "C'mon. I'll show you. It takes two people."

He led Sarah back to the living room. "You sit on one end of the sofa and I'll sit on the other," he said. They both sat down.

"When I say 'Go,' you scratch your finger on your side of the sofa. Then I'll do it," Peter told her.

Sarah hung her arm over the end of the sofa. Peter said, "Go." With one finger, Sarah scratched her nail against the side of the sofa. *Scritch, scritch, scritch.*

Patches came tearing over to Sarah's end of the couch to see what was making the noise. The pupils of her eyes had grown very large.

"Now stop," whispered Peter. Sarah stopped.

*Scritch, scritch, scritch* went Peter's fingernail on the other end of the sofa.

Patches went tearing over to his end to see where the noise was coming from.

*Scritch, scritch, scritch.* Sarah's side.

Patches went running.

*Scritch, scritch, scritch.* Peter's side.

Patches went running back again.

Sarah's side . . .

Peter's side . . .

Sarah's side . . .

Peter's side . . .

"Land sakes, Peter, you're going to have that cat clean out of her mind if you're not careful!" said Granny Belle. Sarah thought she saw just a trace of a smile on the old woman's face.

Peter grinned. "See?" he said to Sarah. "Going crazy. That's what Patches does best."

Perhaps the problem was solved, Sarah thought. Peter had a pet, and it looked as though he was going to keep her. Granny Belle didn't like cats, but she *might* let the cat stay. *If*, of course, it didn't cause any trouble.

## Seven

# Trouble

The trouble with Patches was that she was a full-grown cat. She already had habits, and not all of them were good.

She liked to walk through open doors. She liked to climb stairs. She liked to follow strangers. Once she got out and followed the mailman to the sidewalk. Another time she escaped to the laundry room.

She meowed outside Sarah's apartment and chased a ball from the fourth floor down to the first. She also almost fell out of a window.

Each time Peter left the apartment, he

46

had to check that Patches wasn't there, waiting to run out. Granny Belle said that when Peter was at school, Patches followed her around from room to room.

"That animal doesn't even know she's a cat!" Granny Belle complained. "She thinks she's my shadow."

Sarah decided that Patches didn't know *what* kind of animal she was. When she wanted something to eat, she almost howled, sounding like a dog. When Sarah and Peter tried to catch her, she ran down the stairs like a racehorse. When she tried to find something between the couch cushions, she dug like a squirrel.

"Patches," Sarah said, holding the cat in her arms. "You are a cat. C-A-T."

"She's a baaaaad cat, that's what she is," said Granny Belle.

"Don't you like her at all?" asked Sarah.

"She messes, she mews, and she gets between my feet when I walk. She scratches the sofa. What's there to like?" said Granny

Belle. "When are you going to find a home for this animal?"

"But don't you love her even a teeny-tiny bit?" asked Peter.

"Only when she's sleeping," the old woman grumbled. "You could get rid of her tomorrow, and I wouldn't miss her at all. The only good thing about her is that we'll never have mice."

Sarah thought about that as she went back upstairs. Mom was painting a picture for a book. Riley was cutting elephants out of red paper on the floor.

"Do we have mice?" asked Sarah.

"I've seen one or two," Mom said.

"With Patches in the building, maybe we won't have any at all," said Sarah.

"That would be good," said Mom.

And maybe Granny Belle would love Patches, Sarah thought.

When her father called that Sunday, Sarah talked to him first. "How can you help someone like something?" she asked.

"Build a bridge," said her father.

"What?" said Sarah. That was *his* work. How was she supposed to build a bridge?

"Who are you talking about?" asked her father.

"Granny Belle and Peter's cat," said Sarah.

"Oh," said Dad. "Well, you have to make a connection somehow between the person and the cat. But you're my Idea Girl, remember? Just think of a way for Granny Belle to need that cat. Once she needs it, maybe she'll grow to love it."

Being an Idea Girl was hard work, Sarah thought. She would have to use her *eyes* and *ears*. She would have to watch Granny Belle. She would have to listen carefully to see if there was some way Peter's grandmother might need a cat.

Peter invited Sarah to come down to play with Patches that afternoon. Granny Belle said she could stay for dinner. Sarah asked her mother, and Mom said she could, but Peter should come for supper on Monday at Sarah's.

Sarah put on a clean T-shirt. She washed her hands and combed her hair. When she got down to Peter's, she could smell roast chicken in the oven.

There was rice to go with the chicken.

There was spinach to go with the rice.

There were beans with ham.

There was even pecan pie for dessert.

Sarah ate two helpings of everything except the beans.

"This is the best pecan pie I have ever tasted," she told Peter's grandmother.

"Would you like another piece?" Granny Belle asked her.

"Yes, please. Just a *little* piece," Sarah said.

She was trying to use her eyes and ears. She noticed that Granny Belle was wearing two sweaters again and a jacket. It was chilly in the apartment. Every time the wind blew, Sarah could hear it whistle around the window frame.

"I wish Mr. Gurdy would turn up the heat!" Granny Belle complained. "It's November already. Does he think we are polar bears?"

"We could ask him nicely to make it warmer," Sarah suggested.

"Yeah, we could take Patches for a walk in the building," said Peter. "Maybe she wouldn't be so curious about it if we showed her around ourselves."

"I doubt that," said Granny Belle.

Peter picked up the cat. Then he and Sarah went down to the first floor. They looked out through the glass doors to the street.

"See, Patches?" said Peter. "See what's out there? If you ever got out in the street, you would probably get run over."

They went on down the stairs to the basement and showed Patches the laundry room. They put her on the floor and let her walk around.

"There's nothing here for you," Peter told her. "Take a good look."

Patches sniffed at everything.

She sniffed at the washing machines.

She sniffed at the dryers.

She sniffed at the laundry baskets and the soap powders.

One of the washing machines suddenly emptied its water in the laundry sink, and Patches jumped, her fur on end.

They took her into the furnace room, where the water heater went *ticka, ticka, ticka*. When the furnace came on with a *whoosh*, Patches jumped again. Her tail thickened.

All at once a loud voice boomed, "What is that cat doing in my furnace room?"

Mr. Gurdy was standing in the doorway, hands on his hips. He wasn't smiling the least little bit.

# Eight

# Cat Stew

"We were just showing Patches around," said Sarah quickly.

"I don't *want* that cat around!" said Mr. Gurdy. "I don't want her in my furnace room. I don't want her in my laundry room. I don't want her in my workroom. And I especially don't want her in the room where I live."

"She won't hurt anything, Mr. Gurdy," Peter promised. "She might even eat your mice."

"Don't talk to me about mice," said the man with the mustache. "I know what to do

about mice. If you want your cat to live a long and healthy life, keep her out of my basement."

"What could possibly happen to Patches here in the basement?" asked Sarah.

"Cat stew with onions and tomatoes could happen," said Mr. Gurdy.

Peter scooped the cat up in his arms. Sarah knew that Mr. Gurdy was teasing, but it wasn't the kind of teasing she liked.

As they turned to go, she said, "Granny Belle is cold up there in her apartment. We can hear the wind whistling around the window. She has to wear two sweaters and a jacket to keep warm."

"Complain, complain, all I hear is complaining," said Mr. Gurdy. "Folks on one side of the building are too hot. Folks on the other side are too cold. If I turn the heat up, people on one side say they are burning. If I turn the heat down, people on the other side say they are freezing. That's why I keep the temperature right in the middle, and there's nothing I can do about it."

When Sarah and Peter went back upstairs, it was hard to explain that to Granny Belle.

"Humph," she said, opening her book. "Easy for *him* to say. He's down there next to the furnace all nice and cozy. If he lived up here, he'd be chilly, too." She adjusted her glasses and began to read.

Peter sat at one end of the couch looking at a magazine. Sarah sat at the other end with Patches on her lap. The cat was purring, and Sarah could feel the purr on her legs.

Sarah looked at Granny Belle, holding her jacket closed beneath her chin. She looked at the curtains fluttering in the window whenever a gust of wind hit the building. And then she had an idea.

"Whew!" Sarah said softly, wiping her forehead.

Granny Belle looked up from her book. Then she went on reading.

Sarah waited a moment. Then she said, "Wow! My legs are getting so hot! Patches, you are like an electric heater. I don't know how much longer I can keep you on my lap."

Granny Belle looked up again.

Sarah went on talking to the cat. "I think if you sit on my lap any longer, I'll need a fan to keep me cool." She stroked Patches' head and behind her ears. "All this thick fur must keep you warm. But you're a little too hot for me."

"Sarah, you don't have to suffer with that cat," Granny Belle said. "Here. Bring her over to me."

"Oh, I don't mind," said Sarah. "It's only a little uncomfortable."

"Nonsense, I'll take her," said Granny Belle. "You're Peter's guest, and you shouldn't have to sit with a cat on your lap."

"Well, if you really don't mind," Sarah said. She gently picked up the sleepy cat and took her over to Granny Belle. She placed her on the old woman's lap.

Patches opened her eyes and licked one paw. Then she stretched out her legs, yawned, and curled up again.

"My goodness, yes, she is warm," said Granny Belle. "Hmmm. Like a little heater, she is. Ummm. Troublesome cat. Making us all miserable." But she began to stroke the cat's head.

Peter looked up from his magazine.

"I could hold her for a while," he said.

"No, no, she's asleep again. I'll put up with her for the evening, but I won't say I like it," said Granny Belle. Sarah tried very hard not to smile.

Peter came over to Sarah's for Monday supper. He also brought his cat.

"Patches is welcome to come for short visits, Peter," Mom explained. "But if she stays very long, I start to sneeze."

"I won't stay very long," said Peter.

Monday supper at Sarah's apartment was leftovers. Mom served:

two slices of pizza
a dish of spaghetti
some applesauce
a cinnamon roll
peas and carrots
a piece of banana cake
a little asparagus, and
Oreo cookies.

Sarah's mother cut the pizza and the cinnamon roll and the banana cake into four pieces.

Peter put a little of everything on his plate, even the asparagus.

"This is the best supper I ever ate," he said.

"Then you'll have to come again, Peter. This is the way we eat supper every Monday," said Sarah's mother.

Riley even gave Peter the pepperoni off his pizza.

They gave Patches a plastic straw to play with. They put a paper sack upside down on top of the cat and watched her work her way out of the bag.

Riley put Patches in a basket and pulled her across the floor. The cat seemed to love the basket game. She also liked the "pull-the-string" game and the "chase-the-ball" game and the "hide-behind-the-sofa" game. She liked sitting at the window and watching the pigeons fly between the two buildings. She made funny noises in her throat when she saw the pigeons. Her jaws trembled. Her tail swished.

When Mom began to sneeze, however, it was time for Peter to go home. Patches was ready for a nap. Sarah followed Peter down the stairs.

"About time you brought that animal back," said Granny Belle. She took the cat from Peter and carried it over to her rocking chair.

Sarah and Peter smiled at each other. Dad was right. Sarah had built a bridge, and the problem seemed to be solved.

But the next day when Sarah and Peter got home from school and started up the stairs with Mercedes and Leon, they found Granny Belle standing in the hall. She had a worried look on her face.

"I'm afraid that Patches is missing," she said.

# Nine

# Lost and Found

"Oh, no!" cried Peter and Sarah together.

How could it be, Sarah wondered, that whenever one problem was solved, another was waiting, even bigger?

First Peter wanted a pet, but he couldn't have any. Then he got a cat, but he wanted a dog. When he started to like the cat, Granny Belle didn't. And now, just when it seemed that Granny Belle was growing fond of her, too, Patches was missing. It would take an extraordinary pair of eyes and ears to find a missing cat.

"I'll help you look for her, Peter," Sarah

said. "Maybe your grandmother just hasn't looked in the right places."

"We'll all help," said Mercedes. "We'll look everywhere in this building."

"We'll even go outside and look," said Leon.

They looked under the beds.

They looked on the seats of chairs.

They looked behind the sofa, the magazine rack, the curtains. No cat.

Sarah felt like crying.

"Could Patches have gotten out?" Peter asked his grandmother.

"I don't see how, but anything is possible with that cat," Granny Belle replied.

"Did anyone go in or out of the apartment after I left for school?" Peter asked.

Granny Belle thought about it. "No, not that I remember." And then she said, "Wait a minute. The mailman brought a package to the door this afternoon. Maybe Patches got out then."

"Come on, Peter! Let's look in the basement!" Sarah said. She hoped it wouldn't be too late. If Mr. Gurdy had found Patches, anything might have happened.

When the four children went down to the basement, they looked in the furnace room, behind valves, and in boxes and trunks. They looked behind every washer and dryer in the laundry room. They even opened the doors to the machines to be sure Mr. Gurdy hadn't put Patches inside. They checked out the workroom where Mr. Gurdy fixed things that were broken. But there was no sign of Patches anywhere.

Sarah went across the hall to the room where Mr. Gurdy lived and knocked. No one answered. Then she saw a note taped to the door:

GONE TO THE DENTIST.
BACK AT SIX.

"What if he took Patches with him?"

asked Peter. "What if he plans to drop her somewhere along the way?"

"He may not like cats, Peter, but I don't think he would do something like that," said Sarah. "Let's keep looking."

Sarah and Peter and Mercedes and Leon went outside and checked around the bushes. They looked in the alley.

"I even looked in the street for a dead—" Leon began, but Mercedes poked him with her elbow and he didn't finish. He didn't have to. Sarah knew what they were thinking. It's what you always think about when you have a cat in the city, with cars and trucks rumbling by all day.

The four friends went up the stairs to the loft. Sarah's mother didn't look very happy, either.

"I'm afraid this isn't a good day for cocoa," she said, blowing her nose. "I think I'm coming down with a cold. I've got a headache, and Riley is playing his CD player much too loud."

Then she noticed their faces. "Oh, dear," she said. "It doesn't look like it's a good day for you, either. What's wrong?"

"We're sad," Sarah told her. "Patches is missing."

"What?" said Mom. "Oh, no!"

"We've looked everywhere," said Peter. "I'm afraid someone might have found her by the front door. Maybe they let her out by mistake."

"I'm so sorry," said Mom.

"Can we look around to see if she could be in here?" asked Sarah.

"Of course you can, but I haven't seen her all day," said Mom. She sat down in a chair and put one hand to her aching forehead.

Sarah and her friends checked everywhere in the loft. They even checked out Riley's toy chest. All the while, Riley sat on the big sofa, listening to band music on his little CD player.

Sarah looked around. She carefully used her eyes and her ears. Something was not quite right. Riley was too quiet. The music was too loud. Mom was too crabby. What could it be?

"Riley!" Mom said crossly. "Would you *please* turn that music down! My head is splitting!"

Riley looked at Mom. He looked at Sarah. Finally he picked up his CD player and turned the music down. Mom sneezed.

And then Sarah heard it. A loud *meow* from the coat closet.

"Aha!" Sarah cried. She ran to open the closet door. There was Patches, her tail swishing angrily. She marched out of the closet and sat down in the middle of the floor.

"Patches!" everyone cried.

Mom sneezed again. "Riley, how long has that cat been in there?" she asked.

Riley hung his head. "Not very long," he said.

"But *why*?" asked Peter. "We've been looking all over for her."

Riley looked as though he might cry.

"When I took the garbage down to the furnace room this afternoon, Patches was there. I picked her up, and Mr. Gurdy saw us. He said if that cat came down again, he was going to make cat stew with onions and tomatoes."

Everyone started to laugh.

"Oh, that man!" said Mom. "He can say the wildest things."

Riley did not think it was funny. "I had to hide her!" he said. "If I gave her back to Granny Belle, Patches might get out again. So I brought her up here and let her sleep on my bed."

Mom blew her nose. "And all the while I was working down at the end of the loft. I didn't know she was up here, but my nose did. How did she get in the closet?"

"You stopped working to make some tea," Riley said. "I was scared if you saw her, you'd make me take her downstairs. So I put her in the closet and played my CD loud so you wouldn't hear her."

"Then why didn't you tell us when we came in that you had the cat?" asked Sarah.

Riley's voice squeaked just a little. "I knew if you saw her in the closet, you'd be mad."

"Oh, Riley," said Mom, laughing. "No wonder I've been sneezing!"

Peter picked up his cat and nuzzled her neck. "Granny Belle will have to be more careful not to let you out from now on," he said. "You can only leave the apartment if you're with me."

"I think with all of us looking out for Patches, she'll be okay," said Mercedes.

"If we see her outside, we'll bring her right in," said Leon.

"Riley will watch for her in our building while we're in school," Sarah said. "And I'll be the Cat Cop when I'm home."

"What will Peter do?" asked Riley.

"I'll do everything else," said Peter. "I'll feed her and pet her and clean up after her and play with her. But right now I'd better let Granny Belle know she's safe."

Everyone wanted to go downstairs to Peter's apartment to tell his grandmother the good news.

Granny Belle was standing in the doorway, looking this way and that. When she saw them coming, her eyes opened wide.

"We found her!" Peter said happily. "Riley was trying to hide her from Mr. Gurdy."

Granny Belle's face broke into a wide smile. She held out her arms. "You come right here, you little rascal," she said to the cat. "You come right in here and keep my lap warm. I missed you."

*Problem solved!* thought Sarah, the Idea Girl. But then, *anything* could happen with a cat!

**Phyllis Reynolds Naylor** has written more than 120 books that are beloved by children. Her novel *Shiloh* won the John Newbery Medal and was voted by children as their favorite book in more than twenty states. It was followed by *Shiloh Season* and *Saving Shiloh*. *The Great Chicken Debacle*, published by Marshall Cavendish, was A Parent's Guide to Children's Media Award winner. Mrs. Naylor lives in Gaithersburg, Maryland, with her husband, Rex.

In addition to illustrating the Simply Sarah series, **Marcy Ramsey** has also illustrated a number of other children's books, including *In Our Backyard Garden* by Eileen Spinelli, *The Story of Laura Ingalls Wilder: Pioneer Girl* by Megan Stine, and *Awesome Chesapeake: A Kid's Guide to the Bay* by David Owen Bell. She lives in Maryland.